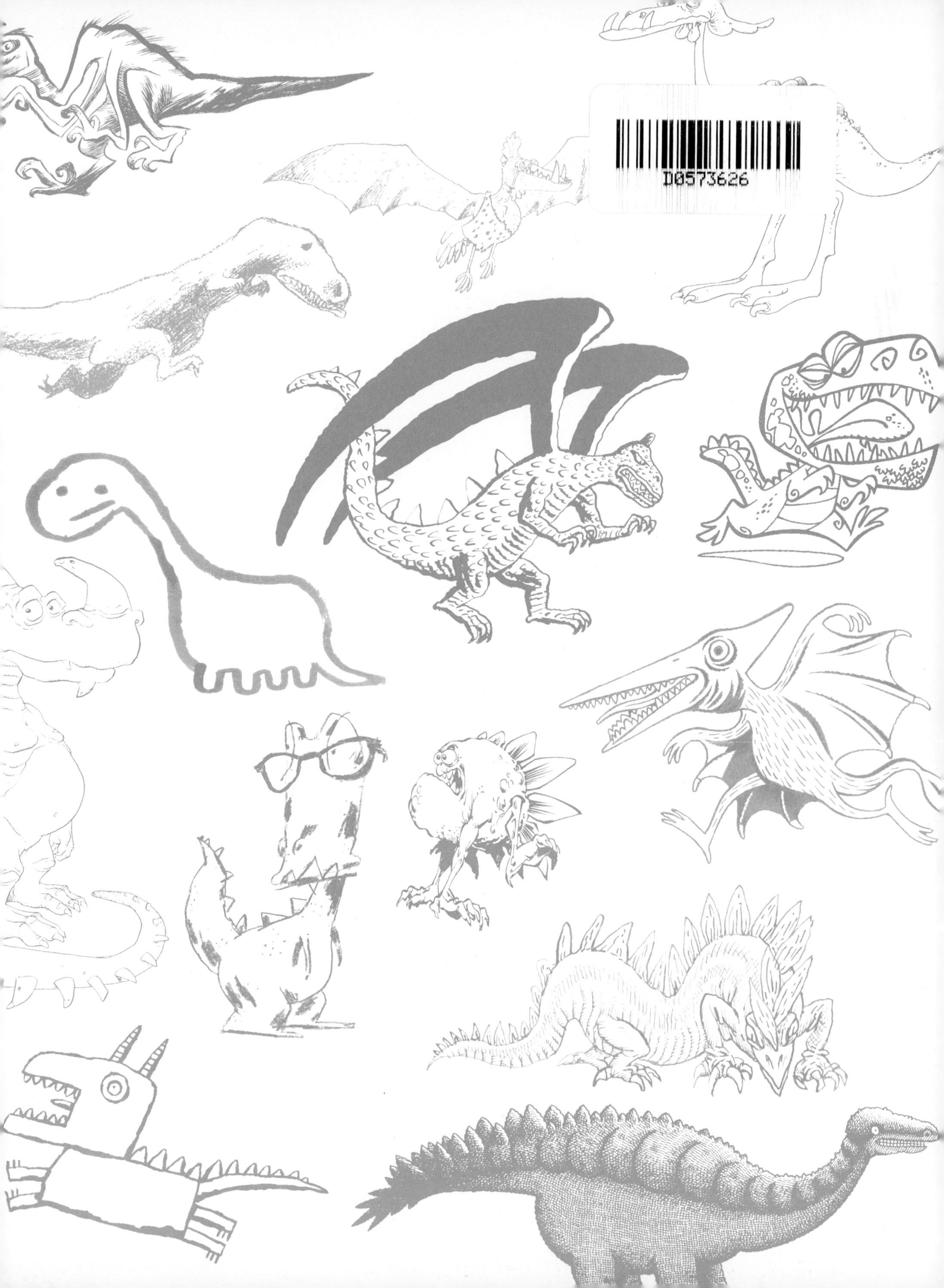

Lewis Trondheim

| Jean | Dad | Kriss | Petey | Mom |

PAPERCUTZ ™

New York

IMPORTANT! READ THIS FIRST!

Petey and Jean love to draw pictures of monsters. One day they draw a scary monster that comes alive—it escapes right off the paper and disappears into their home! Well, they certainly have to do something about that, so they drew a nice monster, with three legs, four arms, and ten mouths to eat the bad monster. The plan works and Petey and Jean decide to keep the nice monster as a pet... and they name it Kriss.

Monster GRAPHIC NOVELS AVAILABLE FROM PAPERCUTZ ™

"Monster Christmas" $9.99
(hardcover only)

"Monster Mess" $9.99
(hardcover only)

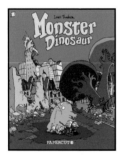

"Monster Dinosaur" $9.99
(hardcover only)

"Monster Turkey" $9.99
(hardcover only)

Papercutz graphic novels are available at booksellers everywhere. Or order from us: Please add $4.00 for postage and handling for the first book, add $1.00 for each additional book.

Please make check payable to
NBM Publishing

Send to:
PAPERCUTZ, 160 Broadway, Suite 700, East Wing,
New York, NY 10038 (1-800-886-1223)

WWW.PAPERCUTZ.COM

MONSTER #3 "Monster Dinosaur"
Originally published as
Monstrueux Dinosaure, volume 4, Lewis Trondheim
© Guy Delcourt Productions — 2000
All rights reserved. English Translation Copyright
© 2012 by Papercutz. All rights reseved.

Lewis Trondheim — Story, Art, & Color
Joe Johnson — Translation
Michael Petranek — Lettering
Janice Chiang — Logo
Adam Grano — Production
Michael Petranek — Associate Editor
Jim Salicrup
Editor-in-Chief

ISBN: 978-1-59707-322-6

Printed in China
January 2013 by WKT Co. LTD.
3/F Phase I Leader Industrial Centre
188 Texacod Road, Tseun Wan, N.T.
Hong Kong

Papercutz books may be purchased for business or promotional use. For information on bulk purchases please contact Macmillan Corporate and Premium Sales Department at (800) 221-7945 x5442

DISTRIBUTED BY MACMILLAN
SECOND PAPERCUTZ PRINTING

Kids games are fun, but
there are too many kids.

And they also
make you thirsty...

We love to play. We like
that best in all the world.

Uh... no... ice cream is
what we like even better
than everything else!

No, wait!
It's dinosaurs!

Once we start looking around, there are tons of dinosaurs everywhere.

It's prettier than when there are just words to get us to buy detergent.

There are even kids with dinosaur balloons, even though we don't have any...

Mom and Dad won't buy us any, so we pout till we get home and see Kriss.

It's too bad he got kicked out of kindergarten because, okay, he just broke a seesaw when falling smack dab on some lady.

While playing around in the garage, we find some papers from the mailbox with lots more dinosaurs on them.

We try to read, but it's too hard.

Since we don't know what it is, we tell Dad we want to go to the movies, or for him to buy us the DVD, or for him to buy us the stuffed animals.

Dad explains to us there's going to be a dinosaur battle in a special arena.

We know dinosaurs don't exist anymore, it's like pandas soon or Tibetans.

So since Dad's telling us something dumb, we go see Mom so she'll really explain the paper to us.

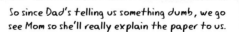

Mom tells us it's a registration bulletin.

Each person can draw a dinosaur on some paper and bring it to life with the shiny powder.

And afterwards, they'll get them to fight in a huge tournament where there'll be a super champion.

We think about it a little and we shout that we want to make a dinosaur, too, so it can fight.

"Bloblo"!

We're going to invent the most terrifying, cruelest, strongest, merciless dinosaur:

But Dad doesn't want us to sign up for the dinosaur tournament.

We say "please," but he still says "no."

We say "please" again, but it doesn't really work.

In cases like this, when Dad's refusing, there's no point in insisting.

We just have to ask Mom.

She says she'll see what she can do and she'll ask Dad why he doesn't want us to.

We eavesdrop and we realize why Dad doesn't want us to. It's because he's already drawn a dinosaur for the tournament.

He says we'd probably get upset with him, if his dinosaur had to fight and win against ours.

Mom says he'd be the one getting mad instead, if it were his kids' dinosaur that won.

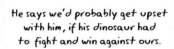

Dad finally gives in, and
everybody's happy except
Kriss, who wants to
draw a dinosaur, too.

Dad tells him that's impossible.
A drawn creature like him
is never able to draw.

Kriss says it's not true and that he's
going to draw a dinosaur anyways.

He takes a pencil, and we see he's
trying really hard, because he pokes
his ten tongues out of his ten mouths.

At the end, we only see some little
lines and we sense Kriss is very sad.

So we tell him his drawing with little lines is the
most beautiful drawing with little lines in all
the world and we hang it on our bedroom wall.

The next day, we head to the coliseum with our paper dinosaur.

On the way, we see lots of people who've brought their paper dinosaur to life with the shiny powder.

Certain ones are very impressive. We wonder if we have any chance of winning.

Maybe we should have drawn Bloblo on an even bigger piece of paper.

Dad comforts us by saying size isn't important.

On the contrary, the smaller you are, the faster you are. And what's more, through winning matches, our dinosaur will naturally end up getting bigger.

There are lots of people signing
up, so we have to stand in line.

Standing in line isn't very fun, especially
since you can't even sit on the ground,
because of all the dinosaur droppings.

At last, we sign up, and the man
tells us to hurry it up because our
first match is getting started.

We wonder who Bloblo's going to have to fight against.

We just hope it won't be against a tyrannosaurus right away...

Once we're in the main arena, a man tells us the preliminary matches take place in the smaller rooms.

Darn... we'd have liked for Bloblo to fight in front of everybody.

In a little room, there's a man waiting for us near a kind of big aquarium.

The gentleman asks us if we're Petey and Jean, with our dinosaur, Bloblo. We answer "yes."

Then a big clamp comes down, grabs Kriss, and puts him in the ring.

We explain to the man that he's mistaken, that he's taken Kriss instead of taking Bloblo.

The man says he's sorry, but that, once a match has begun, it has to be finished.

We encourage Kriss so he'll fight good... or in any case, so he'll run fast.

While trying to climb up the inside of the glass bell, Kriss falls backwards smack onto the little tyrannosaurus.

He's won his fight. The man even says he has the right to eat his opponent, if he wants to get bigger.

Mom says Kriss is already big enough as he is and that he'd risk being too bulky for the house.

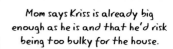

Then the man asks us if we want to exchange dinosaurs, and we say yes.

But Kriss doesn't want to. In fact, he had a lot of fun doing whatever without getting into trouble.

So he's carried off to the following match.

And he won very easily by smashing his opponent...

Next he finds himself facing a stegosaurus that he traps in his mouth and then spits back out after having chewed him.

He crushes a good number like this before moving to the main arena.

We go sit down in the bleachers with Mom and Bloblo. We find Dad there, whose dinosaur also made it through the preliminary rounds.

Dad asks where's Kriss, and we explain to him what happened.

Dad is horrified! He says Kriss was very lucky, because if he'd lost, he'd have been devoured by his opponent.

And he adds sadly that that's maybe what'll happen if Kriss loses the next battle.

At that moment, a speaker announces Kriss's battle against a new dinosaur.

Kriss waves at us, smiling.

Dad quickly goes to the edge of the arena to tell Kriss to withdraw. Kriss refuses, he says he's having too much fun and that this is better than kindergarten.

Dad says it's going to be too hard against the next dinosaur, but Kriss says he's already crushed lots of them and that it's super easy.

Nor even to win against him by running.

But when he turns around, he realizes this one won't be all that easy to crush.

He next tries to climb out of the arena, but he's not succeeding at all.

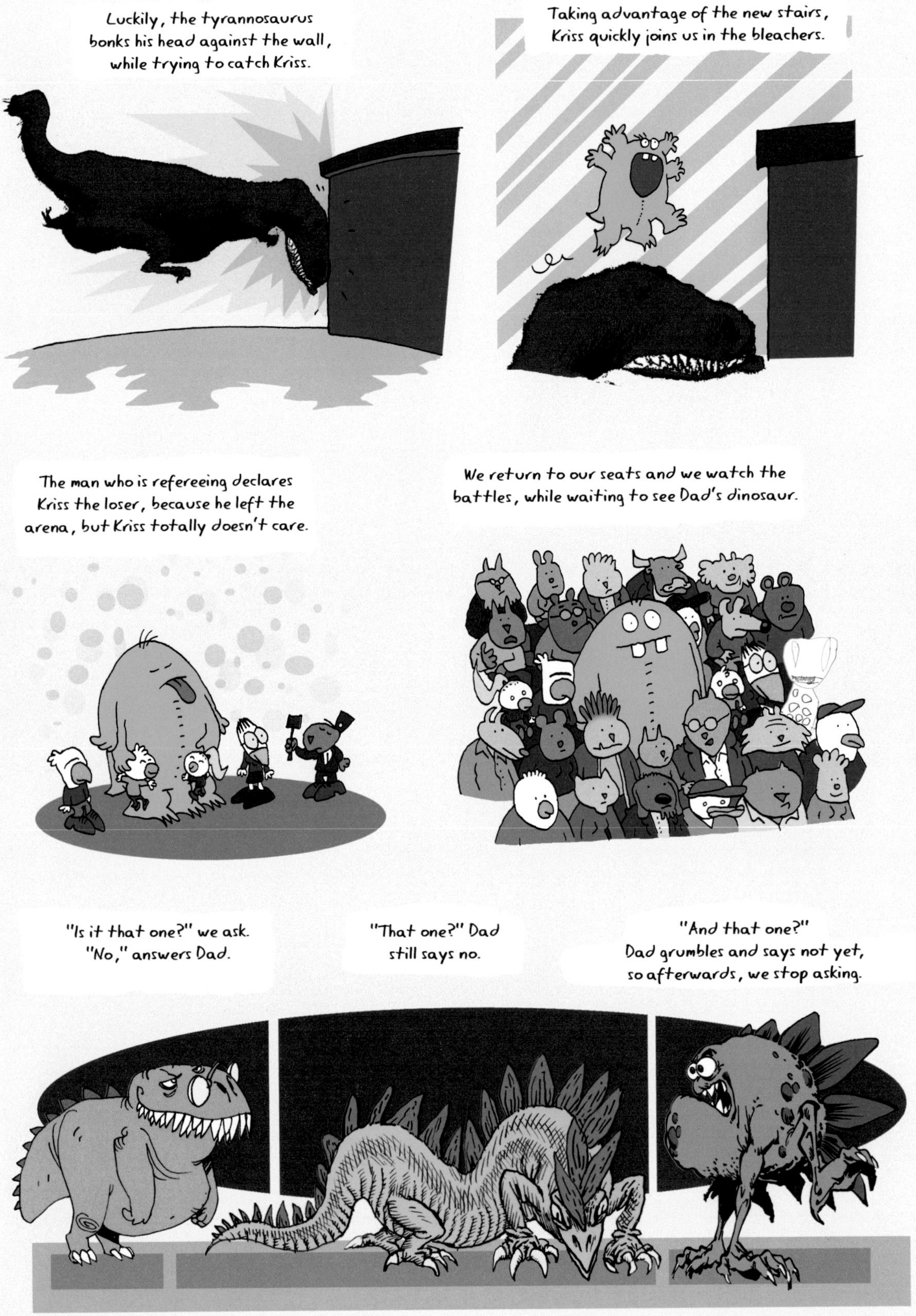
Luckily, the tyrannosaurus bonks his head against the wall, while trying to catch Kriss.
Taking advantage of the new stairs, Kriss quickly joins us in the bleachers.
The man who is refereeing declares Kriss the loser, because he left the arena, but Kriss totally doesn't care.
We return to our seats and we watch the battles, while waiting to see Dad's dinosaur.
"Is it that one?" we ask. "No," answers Dad.
"That one?" Dad still says no.
"And that one?" Dad grumbles and says not yet, so afterwards, we stop asking.

There are more and more terrifying dinosaurs battling...

And since Dad's job is drawing, his dinosaur must be the most terrifying of the terrifying.

"Ah! There he is," says Dad, pointing out a newcomer. "He's gotten a lot bigger than before."

He may be bigger, but he's not very scary...

His opponent looks a little more fearsome...

The battle begins!

Whoa, okay then... Dad's dinosaur has already caught and eaten the other one... We didn't have time to see anything.

Dad explains to us that he didn't make his dinosaur just any old way.

First, he drew and painted the vital organs: the heart, liver, lungs, guts...

Next, he painted the skeleton on top...

Then the muscles, arteries, and veins...

And finally, he covered it all by painting on the skin.

We think Dad drew lots of stuff for no reason.

But Dad tells us, on the contrary, it's very useful. For example, he sketched in retractable claws, like cats'.

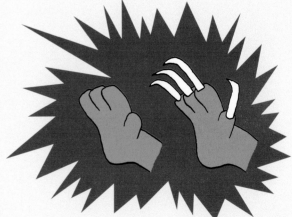

And super strong muscles for its rear paws and jaws...

And very pointy, bony, dorsal plates, also retractable...

As well as venomous glands on the tip of its tail and in its teeth...

And a projectile–tongue like that of chameleons, not forgetting its skin, which can change color to camouflage itself...

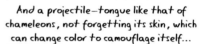

And also some double vocal chords both strident to disorient his adversary and very deep to scare him...

And to top it off, a blinding, toxic spit.

"Whoaaa." We're totally blown away. "So what did you call your dinosaur?" we ask.

He answers that he hesitated between "Terminosauraus," "Assassinosaurus," "Bigbrutosaurus, and finally he chose "Mortalosaurus."

We also suggest to him, as names: "Ieatyousaurus" and "Ibustyourheadasaurus." Dad says they're nice names, but it's too late, he's already chosen.

In any case, his mortalosaurus wins lots of fights and gets bigger and bigger.

At last, he makes it to the finals, where he's going to battle against a megatyrannosaurus.

And that megatyrannosaurus is even bigger than he is.

20

The mortalosaurus starts out by spitting its poisonous saliva.

But the megatyrannosaurus doesn't seem to be very affected by that attack.

Nor by his poisonous tail, nor his terrible roar.

For his part, the mortalosaurus looks very affected by the violent blows of his opponent's tail.

As well as from his kicks.

In no time at all, the mortalosaurus gets completely swallowed up!

We're a little sad for Dad, but he had made it to the finals all the same.

Dad smiles and says he'd won the finals anyhow.

We look into the arena and see the mortalosaurus who's extended his bony dorsal plates, while he was in his opponent's belly.

The mortalosaurus ends the battle by greedily gobbling down the remains of the megatyrannosaurus.

There's a moment of silence before the mortalosaurus who gets bigger, then everyone joyously applauds the victor.

Dad must be really proud of
having won the tournament
and getting so much applause.

But strangely, the
mortalosaurus starts roaring...

And suddenly, he eats part of
the audience and Bloblo even!

Dad feels a little less proud, and the
rest of the audience stops applauding.

Dad tries to reason with his
mortalosaurus, by saying that
doing stuff like that is bad.

But it's not very effective.

We all flee from the coliseum to take shelter...

But the problem is that the mortalosaurus has also escaped from the arena...

And there's no shelter possible against such a monster.

Not even under an umbrella...

Not even in buildings...

Not even by running super-fast.

Just when the mortalosaurus is going to chomp us, we decide to close our eyes real tight.

Then, since nothing happens, we hesitate a moment before opening them again.

The mortalosaurus must have smelled the paper in a bookstore and now he's devouring all the books.

That makes him grow even more.

Afterwards, he starts sniffing the air.

And he runs top speed to a print-shop to gobble down even more paper.

We take advantage of this to go home. That's good, since it's time for cartoons.

But Mom and Dad say we have to pack our bags to flee from the city.

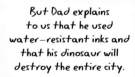

We tell them it's not too serious since, when it rains, the mortalosaurus will disappear.

But Dad explains to us that he used water-resistant inks and that his dinosaur will destroy the entire city.

So we understand and we hurry to save our most precious belongings...

Mom asks us if we were sure to turn off all the lights, but Dad says the mortalosaurus will take care of it for us by trampling our house.

We ask if we'll get there soon, and since Mom and Dad sigh loudly, we realize we'll have to ask the question again later.

On the way, there's an enormous mortalosaurus dropping, so we're forced to turn around.

But afterwards, we get blocked by the debris of houses and a big hole in the street.

Mom and Dad pretend it's not a problem by saying it's not a problem so as not to worry us, so we pretend not to be worried.

Right then, we hear speakers asking all artists in the area to come to City Hall. They want to draw some monsters to fight the mortalosaurus.

Once we arrive at City Hall, we see lots of artists at work.

The head of operations tells Dad to grab a pencil and to draw... but Dad refuses.

He explains he's the one who drew mortalosaurus and that the latter is too strong and too big to fear anyone.

He also adds that drawing monsters too fast and sending them into combat immediately is bad, because you haven't given them enough love and tenderness...

And that's surely the reason why the mortalosaurus went bad.

The head of operations says he doesn't care and he sends the new monsters off to the attack.

Kriss says he'd drawn a super
monster with horns, but
Dad doesn't want to use it.

He says we're going to draw a female
mortalosaurus instead, that way, we could
attract the other one and put them on a
desert isle where they'll stay peacefully.

But the head of operations refuses because,
if it fails, they'll have babies and we'll end
up with millions and billions of mortalosauruses.

So Dad decides to draw a very strong machine
with a grappler to capture the
mortalosaurus and a rocket to carry
it to the moon.

The head of operations
says that that's
totally stupid.

Right then, the artists come back and
say their monsters have been devoured.

So the head of
operations says we'll
try Dad's machine.

We search through the
streets, but we don't
see the mortalosaurus.

Then we look up and
we see him very well.

The head of operations asks if the rocket
will be strong enough to lift the
mortalosaurus, and Dad answers "no."

But he's made lots of photocopies
and, with a thousand rockets,
it'll all be over in ten seconds.

As soon as all the rockets are ready, we send them towards the mortalosaurus.

But with his piercing cry alone, he makes them all blow up at once.

That discouraged us a little...

Then the mortalosaurus started gesticulating in every direction, like trying to capture an invisible monster...

And it collapsed heavily.

Little by little, it disappears while lots of small lines start getting bigger.

Kriss says it's his monster, that he used the shiny powder and that now his monster has devoured the mortalosaurus.

The head of operations insists we give him the monster. He says it'll be very useful for maintaining order at the next dinosaur tournament.

Kriss agrees, provided everyone be nice with his creature. He pets it one last time, and we all go back home.

We ask Kriss what incredible monster he drew, and he answers that it's a fearsome goat.

We explain to him a goat's not a monster, that it's a real animal... but Kriss refuses to believe us.

In any case, it's lucky that goats love to eat paper.

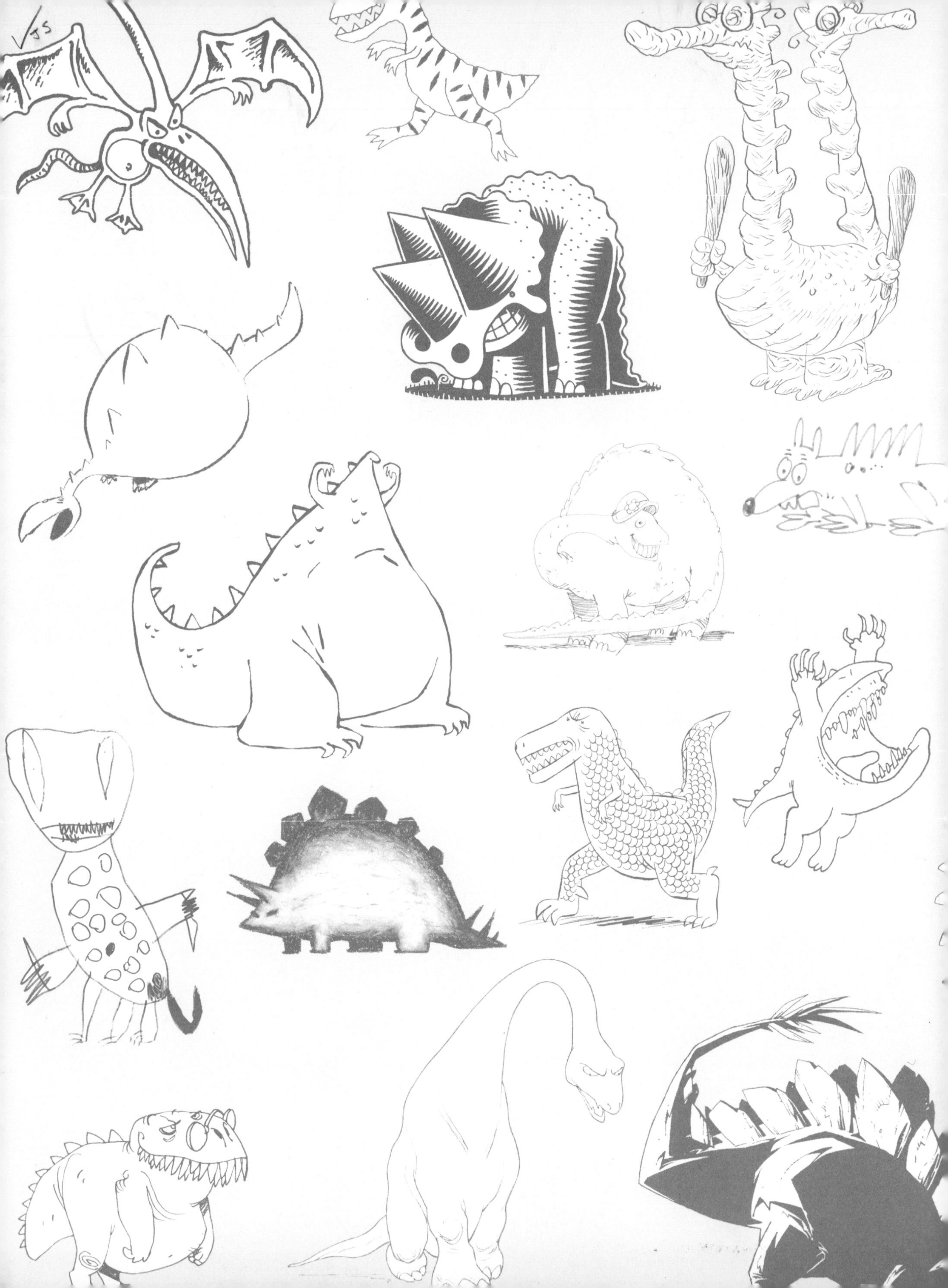
JS